MW00897546

Hello, Bali

A Kids Yoga Island Adventure Book

Written by Giselle Shardlow
Illustrated by Emily Gedzyk

www.kidsyogastories.com

Copyright © 2013 by Giselle Shardlow

Cover and illustrations by Emily Gedzyk

All images © 2013 Giselle Shardlow

All rights reserved. No part of this book may be reproduced in any form by any electronic or mechanical means, including photocopying, recording, or information storage and retrieval without written permission from the author.
The author, illustrator, and publisher accept no responsibility or liability for any injuries or losses that may result from practicing the yoga poses outlined in this storybook. Please ensure your own safety and the safety of the children.

ISBN-13: 978-1492884019
ISBN-10: 1492884014

Kids Yoga Stories

Boston, MA

www.kidsyogastories.com

www.amazon.com/author/giselleshardlow

Email us at info@kidsyogastories.com

Ordering Information: Special discounts are available on quantity purchases by contacting the publisher at the email address above.

A special thank you to Stella Noviani (www.noviani.com) for editing the Indonesian phrases.

What do you think? Let us know what you think of **Hello, Bali!** at feedback@kidsyogastories.com.

Printed in the United States of America.

To my parents, who gave me the gift of travel.
~ G.S. ~

To my father, for being the amazing man he is.
~ E.G. ~

Welcome to a Kids Yoga Stories Book

Hello!

My name is Tia. I'll be your story guide. There's stuff for you to do and follow along on each page. Turn to the sample page on the next page, and I'll show you how it works. I'll introduce you to our Yoga Kid, Anamika, and her family, too.

Don't miss the list of yoga poses and the parent-teacher guide. Learn a little basic Indonesian, too!

How to use this yoga book:

Meet our Yoga Kid, Anamika!
She's from Rajasthan, India. In this book,
Anamika and her family travel to Bali
on vacation.

See the keyword in dark letters? There's one on each page. There's a yoga pose to match it, too. Try it yourself!

The **sun** shines rays of light on Bali.

Hello, sun.

read this!

try this!

Extended Mountain Pose

The **sun** shines rays of light on Bali.

Hello, sun.

Extended Mountain Pose

Surfers ride the rolling waves.

Hello, surfers.

Warrior 2 Pose

Sailboats line up along the bright horizon.

Hello, sailboats.

Triangle Pose

Swimmers slip into the cool ocean.

Hello, swimmers.

Warrior 3 Pose

Dancers practice in the morning light.

Hello, dancers.

Dancing Ganesha

Shopkeepers whiz by on flashy scooters.

Hello, shopkeepers.

Chair Pose

Waterfalls spill into blue pools.

Hello, waterfalls.

Standing Forward Bend

Mountains overlook
this tropical island.

Hello, mountains.

Downward-Facing Dog Pose

Villagers visit their peaceful temple.

Hello, villagers.

Hero Pose

Dolphins splash in the sparkling water.

Hello, dolphins.

Dolphin Pose

Farmers plant in their muddy rice fields.

Hello, farmers.

Squat Pose

Monkeys groom their cuddly babies.

Hello, monkeys.

Cobbler's Pose

Children bike home from their village school.

Hello, children.

Knees To Chest Pose

Statues sit in the still gardens.

Hello, statues.

Easy Pose

Sunbathers bask in the afternoon sun.

Hello, sunbathers.

Resting Pose

Hello, Bali.

What a beautiful place you are!

List of Kids Yoga Poses

The following list is intended as a guide only. Please encourage the children's creativity while ensuring their safety.

KEYWORD	YOGA POSE	DEMONSTRATION
1. Sun	Extended Mountain Pose	
2. Surfers	Warrior 2 Pose	
3. Sailboats	Triangle Pose	
4. Swimmers	Warrior 3 Pose	
5. Dancers	Dancing Ganesha	
6. Shopkeepers	Chair Pose	

KEYWORD	YOGA POSE	DEMONSTRATION
7. Waterfall	Standing Forward Bend	
8. Mountain	Downward-Facing Dog Pose	
9. Villagers	Hero Pose	
10. Dolphins	Dolphin Pose	
11. Farmers	Squat Pose	
12. Monkeys	Cobbler's Pose	
13. Children	Knees to Chest	

KEYWORD	YOGA POSE	DEMONSTRATION
14. Statue	Easy Pose	
15. Sunbathers	Resting Pose	

For descriptions of the yoga poses, please visit www.kidsyogastories.com/kids-yoga-poses.

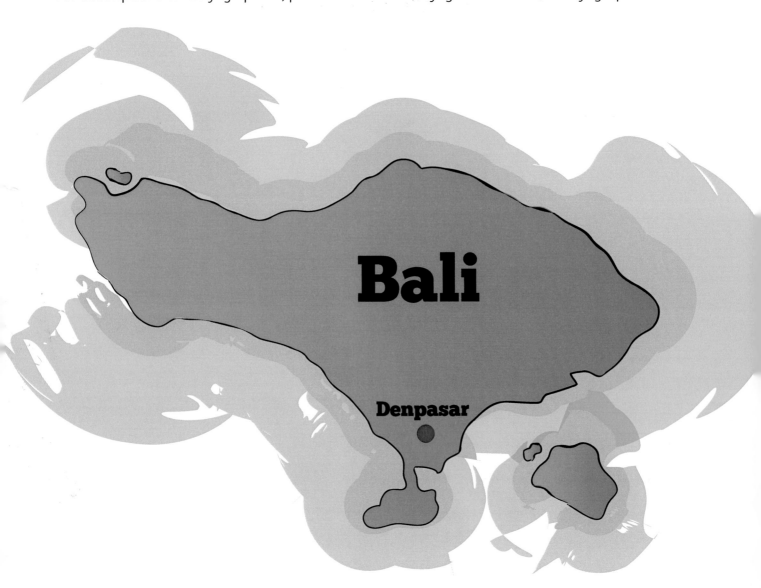

Basic Indonesian

ENGLISH	INDONESIAN	ENGLISH	INDONESIAN
1	→ Satu	11	→ Sebelas
2	→ Dua	12	→ Dua belas
3	→ Tiga	13	→ Tiga belas
4	→ Empat	14	→ Empat belas
5	→ Lima	15	→ Lima belas
6	→ Enam	16	→ Enam belas
7	→ Tujuh	17	→ Tujuh belas
8	→ Delapan	18	→ Delapan belas
9	→ Sembilan	19	→ Sembilan belas
10	→ Sepuluh	20	→ Dua puluh

ENGLISH	INDONESIAN		ENGLISH	INDONESIAN

Hello. → Halo.

How are you? → Apa kabar?

Good, thank you. → Baik, terima kasih.

Good morning. → Selamat pagi.

Good afternoon. → Selamat siang.

Good night. → Selamat malam.

No, thank you. → Tidak, terima kasih.

My name is… → Nama saya…

See you later. → Sampai jumpa.

Have a nice trip. → Selamat jalan.

Enjoy your meal. → Selamat makan.

Welcome. → Selamat datang.

Parent-Teacher Guide

This guide is intended for children's yoga teachers, primary school teachers, early childhood educators, parents, caregivers, homeschoolers, librarians, or grandparents—anyone who would like to experience the joy of yoga with young children.

Put safety first. Ensure that the space is clear and clean. Spend some time clearing any dangerous objects or unnecessary items. A suitable space could be a classroom, school gymnasium, yoga studio, park, or your living room. Wear comfortable clothing and practice barefoot. Wait one to two hours after eating before practicing yoga.

Props are welcome. Lay out yoga mats for children in the pattern that works for the space. Mats arranged in a circle seem to work best for younger age groups. Make sure that every child can see you. Towels could also be used as yoga mats on a non-slip surface. Balinese-related props and Balinese music are a good addition.

Cater to the age group. Use this **Kids Yoga Stories** book as a guide, but make adaptations according to the age of your children. Feel free to lengthen or shorten your journey to ensure that your children are fully engaged throughout your time together. Be aware of any physical or mental challenges that the children or a single child brings to the session and make appropriate adaptations to the poses. Focus on the strengths of the children.
Our recommendation is to read the book with children ages two to five (toddlers to early primary). Break the journey down into a few poses for each session if you are working with ages two to four. Add more poses or extend the ideas if you're working with children over four years old. They might make up their own stories, invent their own poses, read books about Bali, take pictures of themselves in the poses, or paint pictures of the poses and keywords.

Talk together. Engage your children in the book's topic. Talk about the keywords or traveling to different places so they can form meaningful connections. Explain the purpose, set expectations, and review the guidelines for the session. Be consistent and clear in your communication. This helps to set the tone, builds memory skills, and makes them feel safe and secure.

Learn through movement. Brain research shows that we learn best through physical activity. Our bodies are designed to be active. Encouraging your children to act out the keywords not only allows them to have fun, but also helps them learn about different places and techniques for active relaxation. Use repetition to engage the children and help them learn the movements. Ask the children to say or predict the next pose of the journey to Bali. Have them research Bali and find other people, places, or things that they can act out together.

Lighten up and enjoy yourselves. A children's yoga experience is not as formal as an adult class. Encourage the children to use their creativity and provide them time to explore the postures. Avoid teaching perfectly aligned poses. The journey is intended to be joyful and fun. Your children feed off your passion and enthusiasm. Take the opportunity to energize yourself, as well. Read and act out the book together as a way to connect with each other. Whether it is two siblings or cousins, a grandparent and a grandchild, a teacher and a student, or a parent and a child, that connection is important. Bond with the little people in your life. Cherish the moment. Live in the present.

Develop breath awareness. Throughout the practice, feel free to bring attention to the action of inhaling and exhaling in a light-hearted way. For example, encourage the children to make a whooshing sound to imitate the wind moving a sailboat. Take deep breaths when you are resting in the Hero Pose and Easy Pose.

Relax. Allow your children time to end their session in Resting Pose for five to ten minutes. Massage their feet during or after their relaxation period. Relaxation techniques give children a way to deal with stress. Reinforce the benefits and importance of quiet time for their minds and bodies. Introduce meditation, which can be as simple as sitting quietly for a couple of minutes, as a way to bring stillness to their highly stimulated lives.

Ooze creativity, imagination, and abundance. Encourage each child to tap into his or her own creativity and imagination through movement and breath. Use the book as a springboard to other engaging learning activities. Welcome quiet times for reflection. Pause often. Remember, it's not at the end, but during the journey, where miracles happen.

About Kids Yoga Stories

We hope that you enjoyed your **Kids Yoga Stories** experience.

Visit our website, www.kidsyogastories.com, to:

Receive updates. For updates, contest giveaways, articles, and activity ideas, sign up for our **Kids Yoga Stories Newsletter.**

Connect with us. Please share with us about your yoga journey. Send us pictures of yourself practicing the poses or reading the story. Describe your journey on our social media pages (Facebook, Pinterest or Twitter).

Check out free stuff. Read our articles on books, yoga, parenting, and travel. Download one of our kids yoga lesson plans or coloring pages.

Read or write a review. Read what others have to say about our books or post your own review on Amazon or on our website. We'd love to hear how you enjoyed this book.

Thank you for your support in spreading our message of integrating learning, movement and fun.

Giselle
Kids Yoga Stories

www.kidsyogastories.com
info@kidsyogastories.com
www.facebook.com/kidsyogastories
www.pinterest.com/kidsyogastories
www.twitter.com/kidsyogastories
www.amazon.com/author/giselleshardlow

About the Author

Giselle Shardlow draws from her experiences as a teacher, traveler, mother, and yogi to write her yoga-inspired children's books. This story was inspired by her unforgettable travels to Bali and her desire to share these experiences with her daughter. She lives in Boston with her husband and daughter.

About the Illustrator

Emily Gedzyk is a world traveler who draws her artistic inspiration from the places she's visited and the people in her life. She hopes to continue her journeys to new, exciting places and to teach everyone she meets that it's never too early or too late to go out into the world on their own adventures.

Other Yoga Stories by Giselle Shardlow

Sophia's Jungle
Adventure

Good Night,
Animal World

Luke's Beach Day

Sophia's Jungle
Adventure
Coloring Book

The ABC's of
Australian Animals

Anna and her
Rainbow-Colored
Yoga Mats

Many of the books above are available in
Spanish and eBook format.

www.kidsyogastories.com

Enjoy this coloring page from the complementary bedtime yoga book:

Good Night, Animal World

31934750R00031

Made in the USA
San Bernardino, CA
23 March 2016